D0600594

For Hazel Elizabeth Brown, with dogged devotion
—J. S.

For Selkye, my most favorite hound from the pound
—J. M.

Clarion Books is an imprint of HarperCollins Publishers.

The Hound from the Pound
Text copyright © 2007 by Jessica Swaim
Illustrations copyright © 2007 by The Estate of Jill McElmurry
All rights reserved. Manufactured in Italy. No part of this book may be used or
reproduced in any manner whatsoever without written permission except in the
case of brief quotations embodied in critical articles and reviews. For information
address HarperCollins Children's Books, a division of HarperCollins Publishers,
195 Broadway, New York, NY 10007.
www.harpercollinschildrens.com

Library of Congress Cataloging-in-Publication Data has been applied for.

ISBN 978-0-35-862220-8

This book was set in Museo Slab.
The illustrations were done in gouache.

22 23 24 25 26 RTLO 10 9 8 7 6 5 4 3 2 1

Originally published by Candlewick Press in 2007.

Swaim, Jessica.
The hound from the pound /
2007.
33305254651072
mi   03/23/23

The HOUND from the POUND

Jessica Swaim

ILLUSTRATED BY Jill McElmurry

Clarion Books

An Imprint of HarperCollinsPublishers

In Manchester Square, in a cottage of stone,
Miss Mary Lynn MacIntosh lived all alone.
The bedroom was cozy, the kitchen was clean,
but the days were too dreary, too doggone routine.

"I'm lonely," said Mary, who'd reached her wits' end.
"Perhaps what I need is a four-legged friend."
She hurried away to the neighborhood pound,
where Sam, Canine Trainer, showed Mary around.

"All of the dogs are obedience-trained,
except the blue basset," Sam kindly explained.
One look in Blue's eyes made Miss Mary's heart break.
She trotted him home . . . what an *arf*-ful mistake!

While Mary was fixing an afternoon treat,
Blue wandered around with his four muddy feet.
He chewed Mary's bathrobe and peed in her shoe,
then lifted his muzzle and hollered *AH-ROOooo!*

The panters,
    the pointers,
the givers of licks,
    the newspaper getters,
the fetchers of sticks,
    the mischievous, marvelous
mutts from the pound
    burst from their cages
and followed the sound.

AH-ROOooo!

Greyhounds and whippets raced in from the street,
knocking poor Mary right off of her feet.
Siberian huskies blew in with their sled.
Bulldogs and Bedlingtons bounced on the bed.

A Pekingese played tug-of-war with a pug.
Dalmatians unraveled the polka-dot rug.
An Old English sheepdog chased after his sheep,
who counted themselves till they all fell asleep.

Retrievers lined up at the toilet to drink.

Chihuahuas swam laps (*¡muy bien!*) in the sink.

A bloodhound got gummy bears stuck in his snout.

Shar-peis used the shower to steam wrinkles out.

"Help!" Mary cried, "I can't keep all these pets!"
as in walked a dachshund with eight wienerettes—
two dainty daughters and six sturdy sons,
with wiener-dog faces and wiener-dog buns.

The yippers,
　the yappers,
the lappers of bowls,
　the afternoon nappers,
the diggers of holes,
　the mischievous, marvelous
mutts from the pound
　bowed to their leader,
the blue basset hound.

AH-ROOooo!

Arms full of leashes, Sam jumped from his truck,
a sign to the dogs that they'd run out of luck.
Beagles and boxers hid under the bed.
Terriers trembled, and pointers played dead.

Blue gazed at Mary with sorrowful eyes,
breaking her heart with his pitiful cries.
"Sam, I can't possibly part with them now.
I know I can train them. Will you show me how?"

Sam demonstrated the tricks of the trade.
Hot diggety dog, what a difference it made!
The setters, the wetters—oh, yes, even Blue!—
showed Mary what pawsitive things they could do.

A mutt fetched some daisies. A Jack Russell brought tea.
A Newfoundland rested his head on her knee.
With dogged devotion, the rest fell in line.
"Splendid!" said Mary. "We'll get along fine."

The sitters,
      the stayers,
the catchers of balls,
      the hide-and-seek players,
the bouncers off walls,
      the mischievous, marvelous
mutts from the pound
      couldn't believe what
a good home they'd found.

AH-ROOooo!

Sam stayed for supper of hot shepherd's pie.
Too quickly for Mary, the evening passed by.
What started as puppy love rapidly grew,
by leaps and by bounds overtaking the two . . .

Till one golden morning Sam dropped to his knee.

"Mary, my pet, will you please marry me?"

"No bones about it, Sam, I'll be your wife,

to have and to hold for the rest of your life."

The wedding took place by the Chesapeake Bay
at Saint Bernard's Chapel, the middle of May.
Poodles of honor wore gowns from Paree
and ribbons of pink—*ooh la la* and *oui, oui!*

Barking "Sit! Stay!" to the furred congregation,
the minister read from the Book of Dalmatian.
Best man, of course, was none other than Blue,
who howled with delight when the two said, "I do."

The heelers,
        the squealers,
the wearers of bows,
        the tennis-shoe stealers,
the warmers of toes,
        the mischievous, marvelous
mutts from the pound
        echoed the joy
of the blue basset hound.

AH-ROOooo!

AH-ROOooo!